W9-BCR-445

CPS-MORRILL SCHOOL LIBRARY
3 4880 05000893 2
E MED
Just Teenie

DATE DUE			

Susan Meddaugh

JUST TEENIE

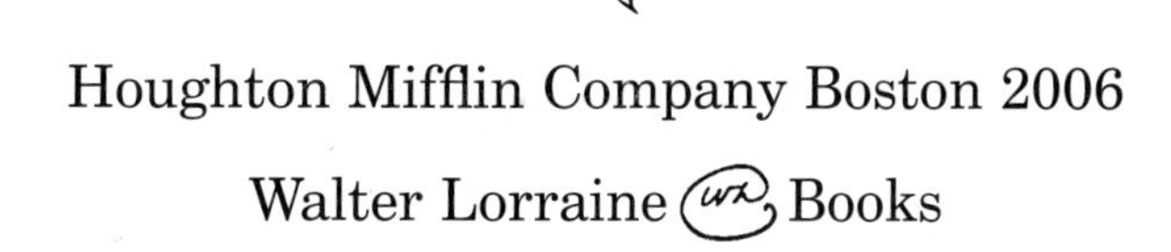

Houghton Mifflin Company Boston 2006

Walter Lorraine Books

For my mother

Walter Lorraine Books

www.houghtonmifflinbooks.com

Library of Congress Cataloging-in-Publication Data

Meddaugh, Susan.
Just Teenie / by Susan Meddaugh.
p. cm.
"Walter Lorraine Books."
Summary: Justine is so small, everyone calls her just Teenie, but one day she receives a plant that grows so tall, it gives her a different perspective.
ISBN-13: 978-0-618-68565-3
ISBN-10: 0-618-68565-0
[1. Size—Fiction. 2. Size perception—Fiction. 3. Plants—Fiction.] I. Title.
PZ7.M51273Jus 2006
[E]—dc22

2005020893

Printed in the United Stqates of America
WOZ 10 9 8 7 6 5 4 3 2 1

Justine was so tiny, everyone called her just Teenie.

Being small was a problem.

"Nothing fits," said Teenie. "Clothes don't fit. My house doesn't fit."

"The whole world doesn't fit!" cried Teenie.

Then Teenie saw a sign.

“I want to grow,” she told Madame Flora.
“As you wish,” said the woman, and she handed Teenie a small box.

Back in her room Teenie opened the box.

"A *plant,*" she said. "I don't want to grow a plant!" She put it on the windowsill and forgot all about it.

The next morning Teenie woke up in a green tangle.

"Outside!" said her parents.

The plant liked it outside.

"I'm glad *something* is growing," said Teenie.

It was the most beautiful plant anyone had ever seen.

And it just kept growing.

But soon small things began to disappear.
Teenie's neighbors were getting suspicious.

And then angry.

Mr. Bolton brought an ax. But as he lifted it to strike, the plant reached down.

The plant grabbed TEENIE!

Up she went over the people,
above the houses,
until she was high in the air,

at the very top of the plant.
"Teenie!" cried her parents.
They looked tiny to Teenie.

Everything looked tiny.

On the ground, no one knew what to do. They couldn't chop down the plant with Teenie on top. They couldn't climb up. They were all too big. "Teenie must be terrified!" cried her mother.

But Teenie looked down at all
the tiny people looking up.
She liked the view.

She decided to stay.

So tiny Teenie towered over the town for the rest of the summer. She swung from the vines and had all her meals delivered by balloon.

At night she slept in a nest of vines,
leaves, and flowers.

Her mother sent up a whistle in case of emergency. Teenie used it the day she saw the Romeros' cat stuck up a tree.

After that people sent her notes whenever
a pet was missing.
Teenie was on top of the world. She was happy.

But cooler weather brought changes.

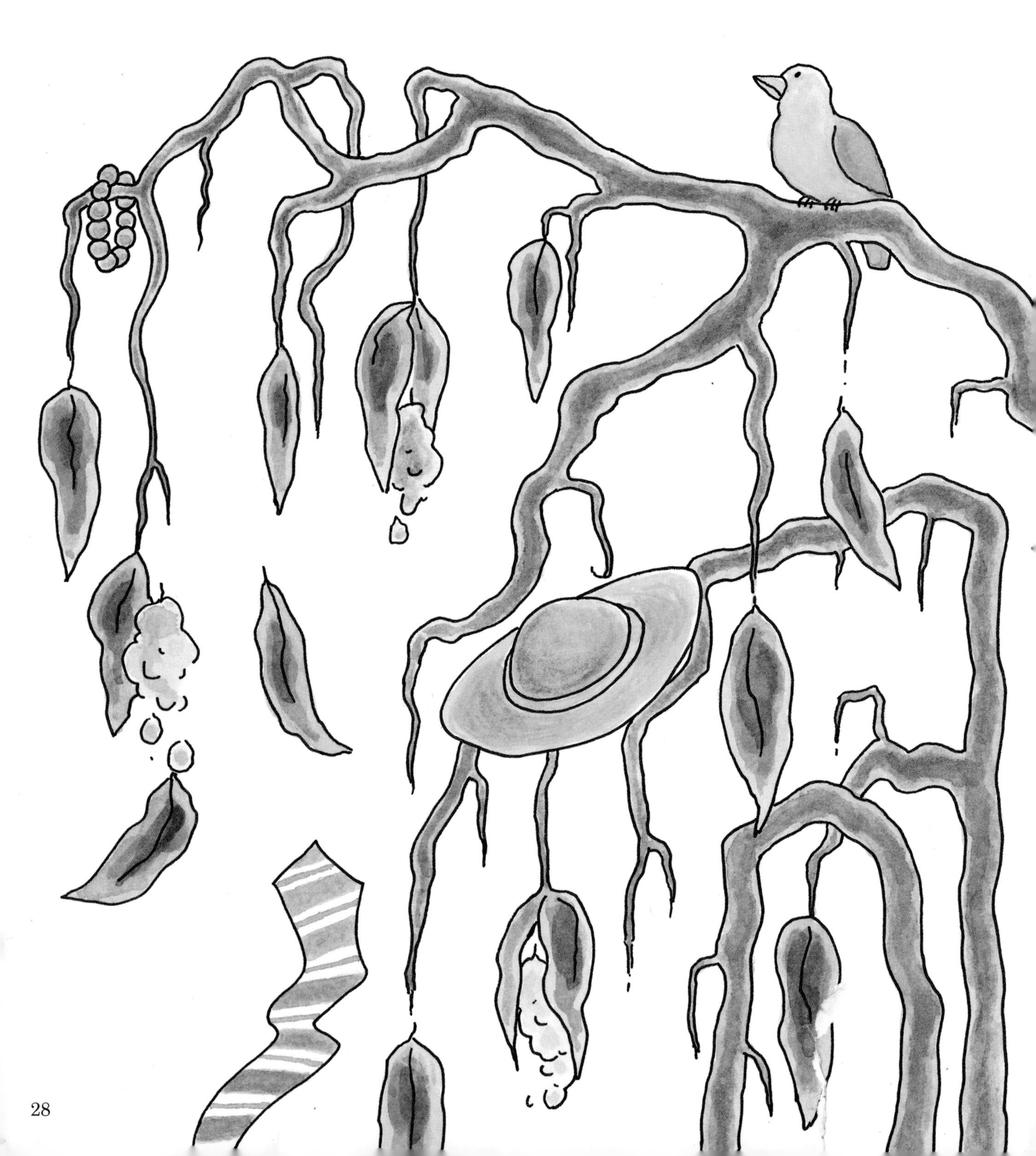

And finally Teenie came down.

She was so sad.

“Find something to remind you of your plant,” her parents suggested.

And that's exactly what Teenie did.
She smiled just thinking about next summer.